The Adventures of Chit C...

BOOK I

FITTING-OUT

This book is dedicated to the memory of
ROB HUGHES
– sailor, adventurer and true friend

The Adventures of Chit Chat

BOOK I

FITTING-OUT

By
CAROLE HUGHES

Illustrations by
ROBERT SCOTT

Chit Chat's Rig

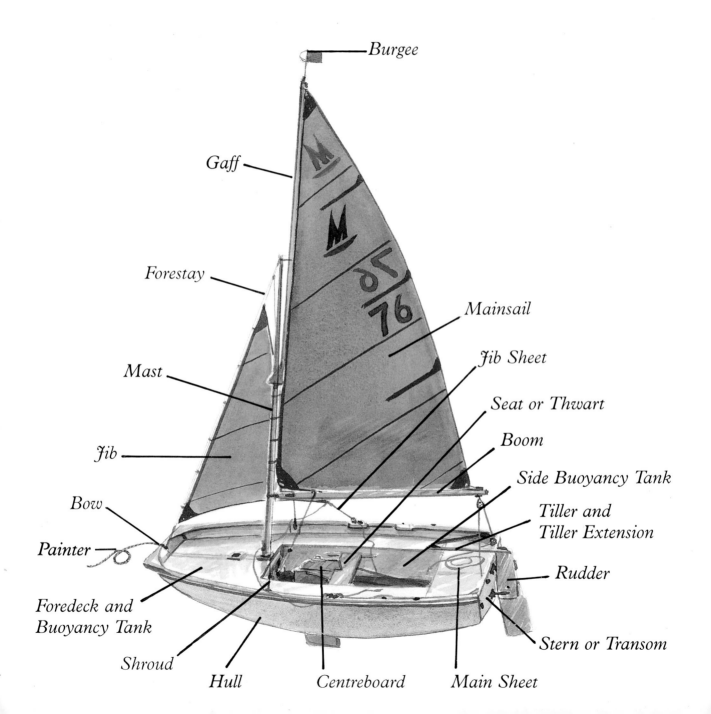

Burgee

Gaff

Forestay

Mainsail

Jib Sheet

Mast

Seat or Thwart

Boom

Jib

Side Buoyancy Tank

Bow

Tiller and
Tiller Extension

Painter

Rudder

Foredeck and
Buoyancy Tank

Stern or Transom

Shroud

Hull

Centreboard

Main Sheet

Harry's wet nose woke Lucy. She was seven and shared the little white terrier with her brother, Tom, who was nearly ten. They lived with their mother in a thatched cottage at Shalfleet on the Isle of Wight. They all loved the sea, especially Tom, who swam like a fish and had a large collection of model boats.

"Tom, wake up, Harry wants to go out!"

Harry leapt off Lucy's bed and tried to peer out of the window, but his legs were too short! It was very early. The dewy mist still hung in the cool air, the birds were in the middle of their dawn chorus and a garden hedgehog was slowly making his way to bed.

Lucy wondered why she felt so wide awake and excited, then she remembered – it was the beginning of the long summer holiday. She decided to wake Tom, who was asleep on the other side of their little bedroom.

"Tom, wake up, Harry wants to go out!" Poor Tom, shaken out of a dream where he was the hero in a battle, was slow to open his eyes. However, having had his face washed by Harry and with signs of Lucy getting dressed, he decided to be a hero in real life too!

"Stop scratching me!" said a creaky voice.

The children crept downstairs, put on their wellington boots and stole out of the cottage. They ran down the quiet lane, scattering some startled ducks, and into the field by the creek. Harry ran ahead, barking at everything that moved!

"Shush," said Lucy, throwing a stick for Harry to retrieve.

The tide was going out and there was a line of wet where the water had laid. Seagulls pecked at the mud and a few small crabs scuttled for safety. Boats bobbed about on their moorings and six small dinghies were pulled up at the side of the creek near several oak trees, which had survived the winter storms.

Lucy picked up another stick for Harry to retrieve and it landed inside a small dinghy with a short mast. Harry, having run after the stick, tried to jump into the boat, but his legs were too short!. He scrabbled at the little boat's sides.

"Stop scratching me!" said a creaky voice.

Everyone stopped doing what they were doing and looked for the owner of the voice.

"That boat spoke," said Lucy, who believed in fairy tales.

"Boats can't talk," retorted Tom (who didn't).

"I can!" said the voice. "Kindly stop your dog from scratching me."

They all gathered around the little boat, which was half full of dirty water and covered with peeling blue paint. Lucy's eyes were like saucers, while Tom still believed that someone was playing a trick on them.

"Well," said Tom, "if you can talk, what's your name?"

"I'm a Mirror Dinghy and my name's written on my transom," said the boat, not in the best of humour.

"What's a transom?" asked Lucy.

"It's the back of the boat," replied Tom, trying to read the peeling letters on the stern. At that moment the boat sneezed.

"Oh dear," said Lucy, "you're catching a cold!"

"We'll bail you out," offered Tom, wondering if boats catch cold.

A bailer can be anything from a saucepan to a plastic jug, but if neither is available a wellington boot will do! So Tom took off his boots, gave one to Lucy and said, rather importantly, "Bail out with this."

It's slow work bailing with a slippery boot, and the mixture of hard work and salt water flying about makes one hungry. Tom suddenly remembered they hadn't had breakfast and, apart from that, his feet were beginning to feel cold!

"I belong to a Sea Captain, so it wouldn't do to sink!" suddenly announced the little boat. The children looked startled at this claim to fame. Belong to a Captain? It was such a scruffy little boat!

"Well," said Tom, "your Captain must have forgotten you!"

Both children were looking and feeling very damp, having thrown a large amount of dirty water over themselves. Harry had just re-appeared, having had a swim. It was definitely breakfast time!

Tom struggled into his soggy boots and having said goodbye to their new friend, they squelched their way home.

"Don't tell anyone the boat talks," advised Tom as they reached the garden gate. After all, grown-ups would never believe such a story, or would they?

After a hot bath and a big breakfast, Tom and Lucy went up to tidy their bedroom and discuss their find.

"She can't be left like that," observed a caring Lucy, cuddling Harry. "We must find the Captain."

They both thought for a few moments then Tom, always full of ideas, decided that Mr Phipps, their friendly postman, would know where the Captain lived.

The village Post Office was a short walk away and Mrs Phipps was behind the counter. The children loved the shop because there was a large jar of jelly babies on the counter and Mrs Phipps loved children!

"Hullo my dears, what can I do for you?" The white haired postmistress peered at them over the top of her glasses.

"Do you know if a Captain lives at Shalfleet?" asked Tom, trying not to look at the jelly babies.

"Captain Crabbs lives at Stable Cottage at the Manor," replied Mrs Phipps. "He's been away for two months visiting his daughter in Australia. Why do you want him?"

The children looked at each other. "His boat's got a cold," said Lucy, always honest.

"It's full of water," explained Tom, not quite accurately!

"Oh, dear!" Mrs Phipps was always sympathetic.

She unscrewed the tall sweet jar and gave the children a handful of jellies –
"Do you think I ought to tell him his boat's sinking?" She laughed at her little
joke.

Tom, chewing hard, wondered if he should explain that the little boat wasn't
always afloat. He decided to ask for a piece of paper to write a message on
instead.

"What did you write?" asked Lucy, as they left the Post Office.

"I asked the Captain to meet us at the Creek tomorrow morning," replied
Tom. "I told him we'd like to help with his boat."

The little boat woke the next morning feeling happy. The sun was warm on her timbers and fluffy white clouds scuttled across a blue sky. She stretched and creaked, startling a seagull perched on her mast. At that moment she saw her new friends running across the field.

"Bother," muttered the little boat, "they've got that scratchy little dog with them!"

"Hullo," said Tom, all out of breath, flopping onto the ground next to the little boat. "Have you seen your Captain?"

"Not yet," replied the boat, "Why?"

"We wrote him a letter," explained Tom, "asking him to meet us here."

"He may not come," observed the little boat, not without good reason!

"Oh!" The children looked at each other. That piece of disappointing news proved wrong, for there was a sudden shout of surprise as Harry launched himself at a stranger walking across the field. He had a grey beard and carried a large plastic bucket.

The stranger picked up the little dog and smiled as Tom and Lucy ran over to him. "Plucky little fellow," he observed as Tom reached out to take Harry.

"Yes," agreed Tom, not sure whether this stranger looked like a Sea Captain!

"Now, what's all this about Chit Chat?" asked the stranger. So that was the name of the boat.

Tom was curious. "Why do you call your boat 'Chit Chat'?"

"It's named after the chiff-chaff, a bird which comes to Shalfleet in the summer and makes a 'chit chat' sound," explained the captain, as they walked towards the little boat.

"We bailed Chit Chat out," said Lucy, eager to join in.

"Very kind of you to help," said the grateful Captain. "I was away in Australia and forgot to ask the boatyard to look after Chit Chat."

"Most unreasonable," muttered the little boat, not at all happy with her owner's excuse.

"Well," continued the Captain (quite unaware that anyone had said anything). "If you have time we could clean off the hull today and when it's dry we'll need to rub it down with sandpaper. As we're going to work together you'd better call me Captain Jo."

The children worked hard all morning, cleaning all the dirt off the inside of the hull.

Then they turned Chit Chat over and cleaned the bottom of the boat. Harry's excited bark was a great excuse for Tom to put down his scrubbing brush.

Cleaning the little boat.

"Harry's chasing something," he called as he went to find the little dog. Harry had found a mole hole and had been half down it trying to find the mole! He was covered in soil and wriggled like an eel when Tom picked him up.

The weather seem to be changing for the worse – there were grey clouds covering the sun and the wind was cold.

Harry was in need of a bath and it was nearly lunch time.

Harry had found a mole hole.

Captain Jo looked at the sky and decided to call a halt to the hard work. "Let's stop now for lunch. If it's fine tomorrow we can start sandpapering Chit Chat's hull and we might have time to put a coat of primer on."

"That's special paint you put on to protect my wood," explained the little boat, suddenly waking up!

"If you both want to paint you will need to wear old clothes. Mud washes off clothes, but oil-based paint doesn't," advised the Captain.

"How long will it be before Chit Chat is ready for sea?" asked Tom, eager to start on the real adventure.

"Well," replied their sailor friend. "We've got to rub the hull down before each coat of paint and we need fine weather for that. The mast, seats, centreboard, tiller and rudder have to be varnished too."

"What's a rudder?" asked Lucy.

"It's a hinged piece of wood which is attached to the tiller and helps steer me," explained Chit Chat.

"The rudder steers the boat," said the Captain, quite unaware that an answer had already been given.

The children helped pack the cleaning things into the bucket and carried Chit Chat's mast to the top of the lane. Then Captain Jo waved goodbye, with a promise to call for them before the painting day.

The next day was wet, so wet that even Harry refused to go out into the garden. Tom and Lucy learnt how to make chocolate fudge cake and then went to sort out some old clothes for their painting job!

It was two days before the weather improved. The children woke, hearing the sound of a gruff voice in the front garden and Harry's watchdog bark. They pulled on their painting clothes and rushed downstairs.

"I have a message for you both," said their Mum, busily frying bacon and eggs. "Captain Jo has gone on ahead to rub down his boat and he's expecting you after breakfast."

It was one of those maybe weather days. Maybe it will be fine or maybe it won't!

Tom and Lucy bolted down their breakfast and, with Harry leading, ran down to the creek. Chit Chat was still upside down on wooden chocks, but most of her peeling paint had gone.

After an hour of hard rubbing down with sandpaper, and a thorough brush to get rid of all the dust, the hull was ready for the coat of primer.

Captain Jo levered the lid off the tin, looked at the sky and said, "Well, if it does rain at least this is only the first coat of paint."

"Get on with it," advised Chit Chat, "it won't rain."

She was right! Within an hour the sun had come out and the air was just right for drying paint.

Tom and Lucy looked as though they had painted themselves, but Chit Chat was beginning to look very smart.

"Well done!" The Captain was pleased with all their hard work.

It took another three days to complete the painting and varnishing. On the third day Captain Jo brought back the newly varnished mast and boom and showed Tom and Lucy how to rig the little boat.

"It's my birthday next week," announced Tom, hoping that his new friend might offer to take him for his first sail.

"Would you like a lifejacket for your birthday?" asked the Captain.

"Why do I need a lifejacket?" asked Tom.

"It keeps your head out of the water if you fall in," replied Chit Chat, who was quite an expert!

"If you got knocked into the water by the boom and became dizzy so you couldn't swim, what might happen?" The Captain was looking very serious.

"You might drown?" replied Tom, not sure of the answer.

"That's right. So you must always wear a proper lifejacket and make sure it's done up before you set sail," advised Chit Chat.

"What if Harry falls in?" asked Lucy. "Do dogs have lifejackets too?" The Captain smiled at her. "Sometimes they do."

It was time to tidy up all the paint pots and clean off the brushes in white spirit (which keeps them soft). Then, having admired the result of their hard work, they left Chit Chat to sleep and went back to the cottage for tea and chocolate fudge cake.

Figure of Eight Knot

To stop the end of a small rope from escaping through a hole.

Tom woke early on his tenth birthday. His Mother had promised a surprise but his greatest wish was to sail Chit Chat. He was pleased to find a pile of cards on the kitchen table and one or two interesting looking parcels.

"Do you think the weather's right for sailing?" asked Tom, trying on his new lifejacket.

"I'm no expert, my love," replied his Mum. "Perhaps we could go down to the creek at 11 o'clock and see what it looks like."

So something was planned!

Tom could hardly contain his excitement while his Mother packed up a picnic lunch for them all.

The children put on their plimsolls so they wouldn't slip on Chit Chat's newly varnished floor and carried their anoraks. It can be so cold on the water and sailors are always glad of extra clothes when the wind blows.

Tom tried on his new lifejacket.

When they reached the field by the creek, they saw Chit Chat at the water's edge with her red sails up! She looked beautiful.

"Happy Birthday, Thomas." The Captain was dressed in red sailing trousers, a navy blue jumper and a yellow lifejacket.

He gave Tom's new lifejacket a tug to make sure it was tight enough, then turned to Lucy and asked: "As it's Tom's special day, would you mind if I took him for a sail first?" Lucy was happy to watch with her Mother.

The tide was coming in. The Captain explained that it's important to learn about tides and to use them when the water is flowing the way you want to go.

"Always make sure you can get back and always carry a paddle and a bailer," advised their sailor friend as he pushed Chit Chat a little further into the water.

"Get in Tom and sit down while I push off."

There were so many goodbyes that Chit Chat muttered, "Anyone would think you were going away on a Round the World Voyage!"

The little boat's sails caught the wind and the water made a gentle slapping noise as Chit Chat slipped through the water. The Captain held the mainsheet with his left hand and the tiller with his right.

"Pull in the jib, Tom," called Chit Chat and Tom heaved on the rope attached to the little foresail.

"I'm going to let the centreboard down as we go into deeper water," advised the Captain. "Remember to keep your head down when we go about, or the boom may hit it!"

"What's 'going about' mean?" asked Tom.

"It's when the boat goes through the wind, you let go the jib on one side and pull in on the other. Let's try!"

Tacking or Going About

"Ready About!"
Captain Jo warns Tom
he is about to tack.

"Lee Oh!"
Captain Jo pushes the
tiller away from himself.

Chit Chat goes through
the wind.

Captain Jo and Tom cross the boat, remembering to duck under the boom. Tom now lets the jib go.

Captain Jo sheets or pulls in the mainsail. Tom sheets in the jib.

"Let go of the jib, Tom." Chit Chat got a bit cross when the sail backed because Tom held onto the rope for too long. Tom found that the adventure of learning how to sail the little boat was even better than his dream.

It's hard work learning how to be a good crew!

After an hour of tacking up and down the creek, he began to understand how the sails work; his hands were getting sore and his feet were a little damp, but it was fun!

Chit Chat, delighted to be afloat again, had begun to sing a little ditty as they returned to the shore:

"I'm on the sea again
The wind and tide
Are at my side
I'm on the sea again."

Then it was time for Tom's Birthday picnic. "I'm starving," he announced, as they pulled Chit Chat's bow clear of the water and tied her painter to a nearby branch.

The birthday picnic was delicious, with chicken legs, crisps, sausage rolls and egg sandwiches, washed down with home-made lemonade.

After lunch there was just time for Captain Jo to take Lucy and Harry for their first sail, while there was still enough water in the creek. Tom loaned his new lifejacket to Lucy and helped push them afloat.

As they sailed down the creek with the tide, Harry, who was over excited, refused to sit or lie down!

"Sit down, Harry," said Chit Chat, a little crossly, for the little dog's claws were scratching her newly varnished floor! Harry jumped up onto the foredeck, but at that moment there was a sudden gust of wind. The little boat heeled and Harry fell into the creek!

"Dog overboard," shouted Captain Jo.

"Keep your eyes on Harry, Lucy, while I tack Chit Chat round." They had been sailing in the middle of the creek and the tide was starting to go out.

Lucy tried to stand up but the Captain laid a calming hand on her shoulder. "You must sit down, Lucy. Where's Harry now?"

"Harry, Harry," called Lucy, anxiously.

"He's swimming for the shore," observed Chit Chat, not at all worried by the little dog's misadventure.

"I think he's going to make the beach," said Lucy, watching Harry struggling against the tide.

"Good, we'll go about again, land Chit Chat on the beach and collect Harry. Help me lift the centreboard, Lucy, so we don't hit the bottom." The Captain was at his best issuing orders, but someone has to be the skipper!

A somewhat subdued Harry was rescued from the beach. Then it was a slow sail back up the creek to where Tom and his mother waited by the water's edge. With the wind behind them Chit Chat could have done with the help of a spinnaker sail, for the tide was now rushing out.

At last they grounded on the shore.

"Did you enjoy your sail?" asked her mother.

Lucy was so excited, she couldn't string her words together fast enough.

"Harry fell in – he barked and barked – then fell in. We had to rescue him . . ."

"We'd better issue Harry with a lifejacket," suggested the Captain, laughing at Lucy's excitement.

They pulled the little boat up on the shore and took off her sails.

Then Chit Chat's crew went back to the cottage for a special birthday tea, leaving Chit Chat to doze and think about all the adventures that lay ahead.